ABC's

of

MAINE

ABC's
of
MAINE

by HARRY W. SMITH

Printed in China

15   16

Down East Books
P.O. Box 679
Camden, ME 04843
www.downeastbooks.com

Dedicated
to
everyone who loves
MAINE

A

Adventurous
Acadia

B

Basket Of
Blueberries

C

Cheerful
Chickadees

D

Dory At
Dock

E
Elegant Eagles

F

Fisherman
In Fog

G

Gliding
Gulls

H

Hiking A
Hill

I

Irresistible
Island

J

Jovial
Jellyfish

K

Kingly
Katahdin

L

Luminous
Lighthouse

M

Majestic
Moose

N

Nimble
Nuthatch

O

Osprey
Overhead

P

Proud
Puffins

Q
Quick
Quoddy

R

Racing
Rivals

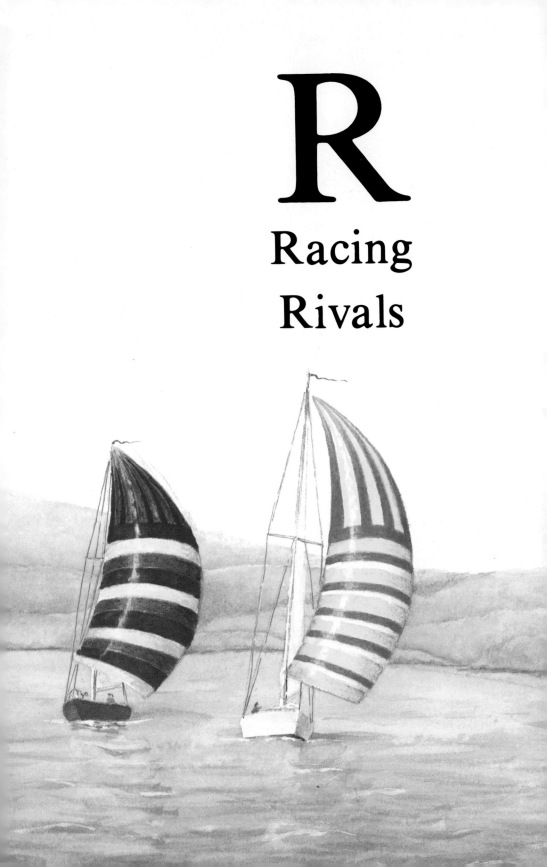

S
Slippery
Seals

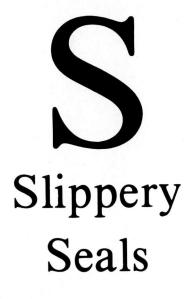

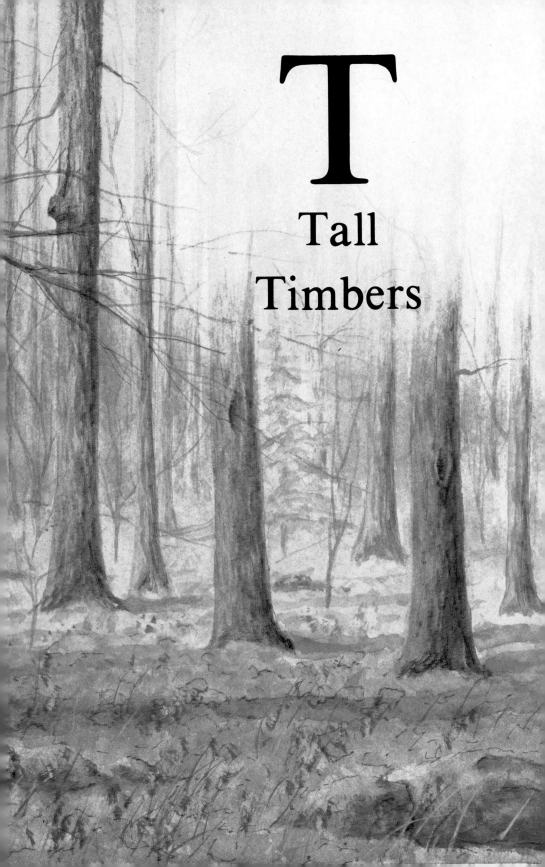

T
Tall
Timbers

U

Unique
Underwater

V

Vivid
Violets

W

Wooden
Windjammer

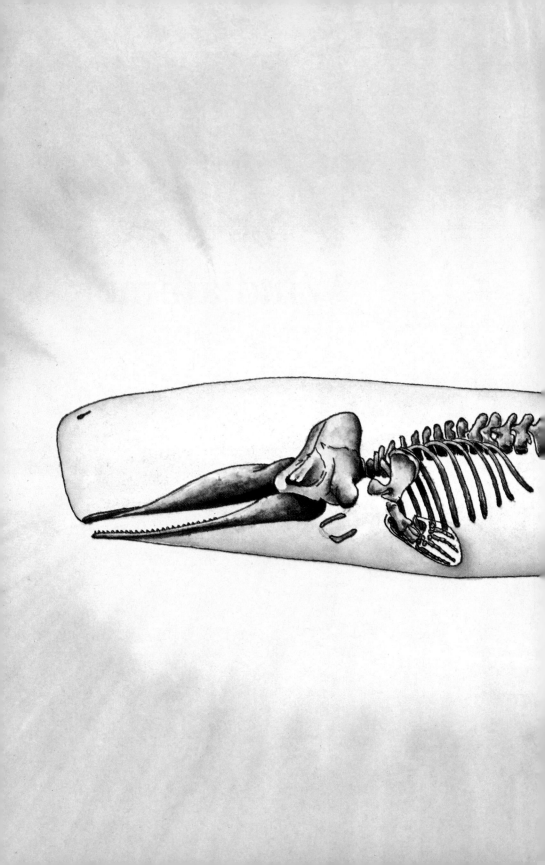

X

XL
X-Ray

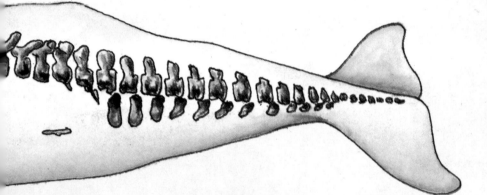

Y

Yankee
Yacht

Z

Zip
Zoom

A - Acadia National Park is located on Mount Desert Island. This picturesque area has scenic mountains and rocky shores.

B - Blueberries grow wild and are harvested by hand in late summer. Maine provides the majority of our nation's blueberries.

C - The black-capped chickadee is Maine's state bird. The pine tree is the state tree and the pine cone is the state flower.

D - Dories are used in many types of fishing. They are often carried on the decks of larger vessels.

E - The eagle is our national emblem. Maine is working hard to help the eagle survive.

F - The coast of Maine is often shrouded in fog. This low hanging cloud makes navigation very difficult.

G - Maine has many species of gulls. These herring gulls often follow fishing boats to eat any scraps thrown overboard.

H - Maine is a hiker's paradise. There are many hills and mountains with special hiking trails.

I - The coast of Maine is dotted with hundreds of islands both large and small. Many have year-round residents.

J - Jelly fish are very graceful. They float in the water with their long tentacles swaying in the tidal currents.

K - Mount Katahdin is located in Baxter State Park. The Appalachian Trail begins on Kathadin's slopes.

L - West Quoddy Head Light marks the entrance to Passamaquoddy Bay. It is located on the most easterly point of land in the nation.

M - The moose is Maine's state animal. Moose are often found wading in small lakes or ponds searching for food.

N - The nuthatch is common in the Maine woods. This agile bird spends much of it's life upside down searching for insects.

O - Osprey or fish hawks have keen vision. They can spot a fish from hundreds of feet in the air.

P - Puffins live in colonies on rocky ledges in the Gulf of Maine. Puffins eat small fish and can catch several at a time in their colorful beaks.

Q - The Quoddy pilot is a fishing boat used in the Lubec area. The Quoddy is similar to the Friendship sloop.

R - The brightly colored spinnakers of racing sloops are a beautiful sight. Boats of all kinds sail Maine's many lakes and bays.

S - The common and harbor seals are found along Maine's shores. They love to sun on rocky ledges.

T - Most of Maine's surface is covered with trees. The northern section of the state produces much of our nation's paper.

U - The waters of Maine feed many people. Fish, clams, scallops, and lobsters are a few of the foods Mainers harvest from the sea.

V - These violets are just one of the many species of wild flowers found in Maine.

W - Coastal schooners, or windjammers originally carried cargo to and from the islands. Now these schooners take passengers on week long trips among the mid coast islands.

X - This x-ray of a sperm whale would be very large indeed. Some whales measure almost 100 feet in length.

Y - Maine's ship yards have been building both pleasure and war ships since Colonial days. J. P. Morgan's yacht, The Corsair was built in Bath.

Z - Skiing is Maine's major winter sport. There are beautiful mountain ski resorts through out the state.